CLEMSON TIGERS

BY K.C. KELLEY

Published by The Child's World®
1980 Lookout Drive • Mankato, MN 56003-1705
800-599-READ • www.childsworld.com

Copyright ©2022 by The Child's World®
All rights reserved. No part of this book may be reproduced or utilized in any form or by any means without written permission from the publisher.

Thanks to Conor Buckley for his help with this book.

Cover: Stephen Lew/Icon Sportswire/AP Photo.
Interior: Newscom: Mark Wallheiser/UPI 9; John Byrum/Icon Sportswire 13, Mark LoMoglio/Icon Sportswire 17; Curtis Compton/MCT 21. Shutterstock: Jamie Lamor Thompson 10, 14, 18. Wikimedia: 4, 6 (2).

ISBN 9781503850323 (Reinforced Library Binding)
ISBN 9781503850576 (Portable Document Format)
ISBN 9781503851337 (Online Multi-user eBook)
LCCN: 2021930287

Printed in the United States of America

A hand off gets the Clemson offense going.

CONTENTS

Why We Love College Football   4

CHAPTER ONE
Early Days   7

CHAPTER TWO
Glory Years   8

CHAPTER THREE
Best Year Ever!   11

CHAPTER FOUR
Clemson Traditions   12

CHAPTER FIVE
Meet the Mascot   15

CHAPTER SIX
Top Clemson QBs   16

CHAPTER SEVEN
Other Clemson Heroes   19

CHAPTER EIGHT
Recent Superstars   20

Glossary   22
Find Out More   23
Index   24

WHY WE LOVE COLLEGE FOOTBALL

The leaves are changing color. Fans are filling stadiums. Pennants wave. And here come the fight songs. It must be time for college football! The sport is one of America's most popular. Millions of fans follow their favorite teams. They wear school colors and hope for big wins.

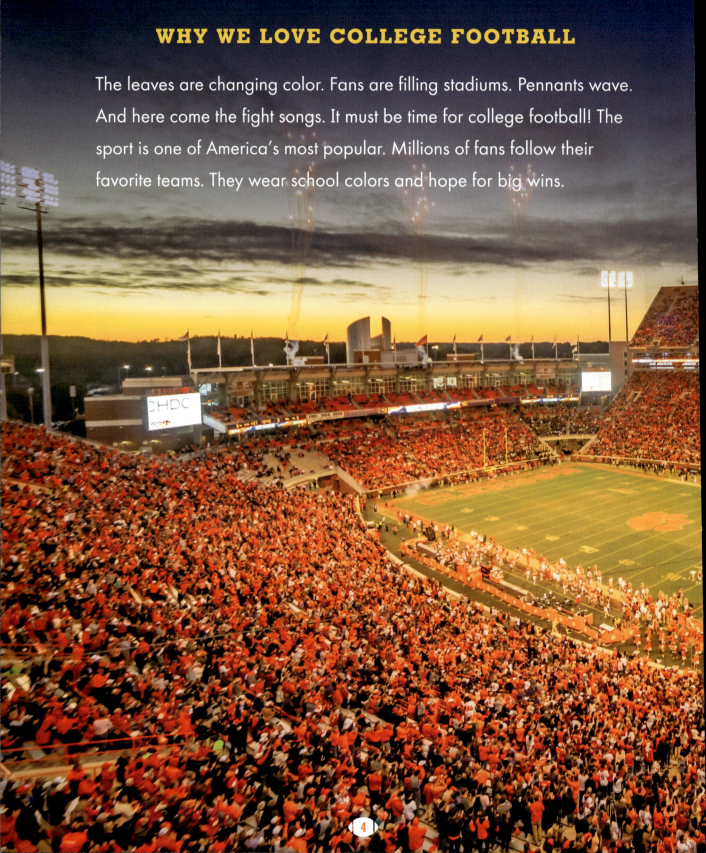

The Clemson Tigers have always been a good team. Recently, they have become one of the greats. Since 2015 they have been in the championship game four times! Fans love to watch their Tigers win.

A sea of orange fills Memorial Stadium for a Clemson night game.

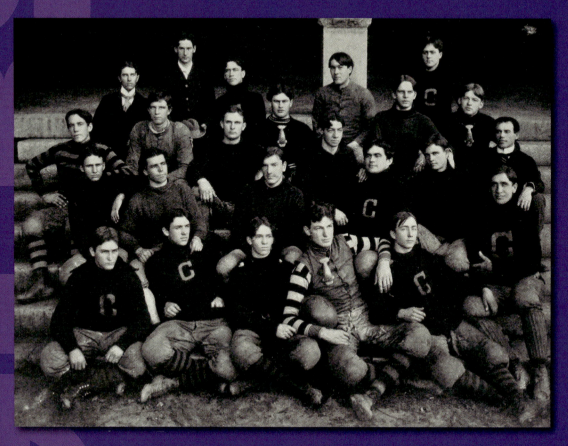

Above: Look at how much rounder the footballs were for this 1901 Clemson team.

Left: The 1903 Clemson team and their coaches and managers.

CLEMSON
TIGERS

CHAPTER ONE

Early Days

In 1889, Clemson University was **founded** in South Carolina. Football at Clemson began seven years later. Walter Riggs was the first coach. In 1897, Clemson beat the University of South Carolina. That made Clemson the state champs!

In 1900, a famous coach took over. John Heisman was the coach of the Tigers for four years. His Clemson record was 19 wins, three losses, and two ties. That is the best out of all Clemson coaches. In his first season, the Tigers won their first game 64-0! That year, they outscored **opponents** 222-10. Heisman became a legend. In 1935, the Heisman Trophy was named for him. It goes each year to college football's best player.

CHAPTER TWO

Glory Years

In the early 1900s, the Tigers were one of the nation's best teams. After Coach Heisman left, they struggled to repeat his success. Then, in 1940, Clemson hired Frank Howard to lead the team. In 1953, the school joined the Atlantic Coast **Conference** (ACC). Howard led the Tigers to six ACC championships.

The next great Tigers team played in 1981. They started the season **unranked**. By the end, they had climbed to the top. The Tigers went undefeated and won the national championship!

In recent years, the Tigers have had some of the best teams. Under coach Dabo Swinney, they won national championships in 2016 and 2018. They have won the ACC title seven times. Through 2020, Swinney's teams were 140–33.

Right: In 2016, coach Dabo Swinney held up the national championship trophy.

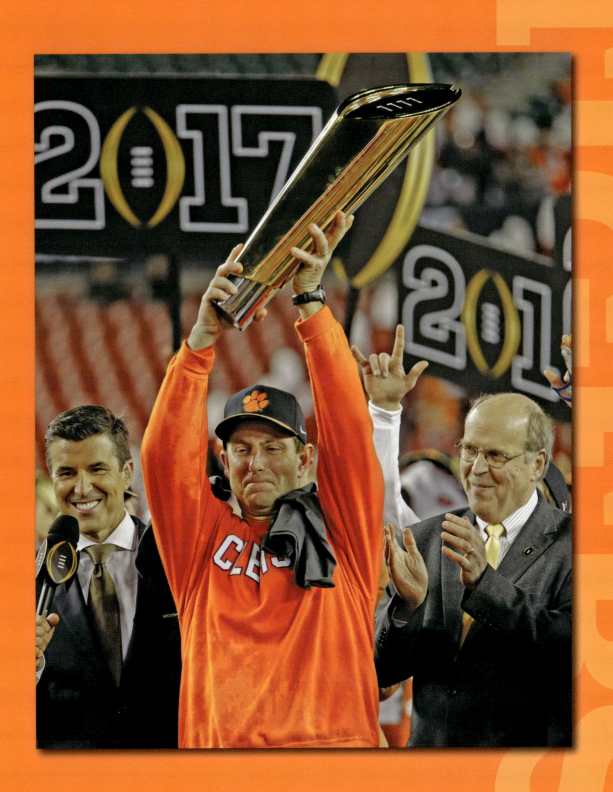

CHAPTER THREE

Best Year Ever!

The 2018 Clemson season was one for the record books! The Tigers began the season ranked number two. They were behind only the Alabama Crimson Tide.

Clemson stayed undefeated thanks to their new star quarterback Trevor Lawrence. They finished the regular season with a record of 15-0. No college team had done that since 1897! The Tigers faced No. 3 Notre Dame in a playoff. They beat the Fighting Irish 30-3. In the national championship game, they faced No. 1 Alabama. Clemson scored 31 points in the first half. Lawrence threw three touchdown passes. Clemson won 44-16. The Tigers were champions!

◀ *Left: Trevor Lawrence had 30 touchdown passes to led the Tigers in 2018.*

CHAPTER FOUR

Clemson Traditions

A football team can't exist for over a hundred years without creating a few traditions. One of the Tigers' oldest is Howard's Rock. The rock was owned by coach Frank Howard. He kept it in his office. Before a 1966 game, Clemson put the rock on a **pedestal** in the stadium. The players rubbed the rock for luck. They won that game! The rock has stayed ever since.

Before each game, Clemson players gather around Howard's Rock. A booming cannon sounds. The team rushes onto the field! The band begins to play the "Tiger Rag." Fans yell C-L-E-M-S-O-N at the top of their lungs! This moment has been called "the most exciting 25 seconds in college football."

THE BIG RIVAL!

College teams often have one big rival. For Clemson, that's South Carolina. They both play in the same state, after all! They first played in 1897. They have met almost every year since. Clemson has won more than 70 times. The Tigers won each year from 2014 through 2019.

CHAPTER FIVE

Meet the Mascot

When Walter Riggs created the Clemson team, he knew they needed a mascot. He let the players pick their own! The Princeton Tigers had just won the national championship. So the Clemson players chose the tiger. They hoped it would bring them the same success.

Today, a student dresses as the Clemson Tiger. After every score, the mascot does push-ups. The Tiger does one push-up for each point in the game. That can be a lot of work! One student Tiger did more than 2,000 push-ups in costume!

> **MEMORIAL STADIUM**
> The Tigers play on Frank Howard Field at Clemson Memorial Stadium. It is nicknamed "Death Valley." That is the name of a place in California that is hot and very tough on visitors! It is the biggest stadium in the ACC. Memorial can hold 81,500 screaming fans!

← *Left: The Clemson Tiger mascot takes a break from doing push-ups to greet fans at Memorial Stadium.*

CHAPTER SIX

Top Clemson QBs

Most of Clemson's best quarterbacks have played in recent seasons.

Tajh Boyd started in 2011. He helped them win their first ACC Championship in 20 years. He holds school records with 11,904 passing yards and 107 touchdown passes.

Deshaun Watson took over in 2014. He is second to Boyd in passing yards and touchdowns. Watson helped the team win the 2016 national title. He was the first college player with more than 4,000 passing yards and 1,000 rushing yards in one season.

In 2018, Trevor Lawrence was just a **freshman**. But he led the team to an undefeated season. They were national champs again! The next year, Clemson was undefeated until the championship game. In the final, they lost to LSU. Lawrence led the Tigers to the college football playoff again in 2020.

Right: Deshaun Watson was all smiles when he held the 2016 National Championship trophy. ▶

CHAPTER SEVEN

Other Clemson Heroes

Clemson's best overall athlete was a football star. James McFadden played for the Tigers from 1937-1939. He played halfback and **punter**. He also was a star in basketball and track. In 1959, he was the first Clemson player elected to the College Football Hall of Fame.

Safety Terry Kinard was another Clemson legend. He was born in Germany, but became a star in America. He played for Clemson from 1979–1982. He made a Clemson-record 17 **interceptions**.

Running back Travis Etienne won a lot of awards. He was the ACC player of the year twice. In the 2018 ACC Championship Game, he was the MVP! He was an All-America in 2020. He also set the ACC career record for rushing yards with 4,952.

← *Left: Travis Etienne might be the best running back in Clemson history.*

CHAPTER EIGHT

Recent Superstars

Clemson's star QBs needed amazing wide receivers. Three of those pass-catchers have become NFL stars.

DeAndre Hopkins is one of the NFL's best receivers. He played with Tajh Boyd. They teamed up to win the ACC title. In the NFL, Hopkins has been named to five **Pro Bowls**.

Sammy Watkins played with Boyd and Hopkins. They formed a powerful passing attack. Watkins broke many Clemson records. He was just the fourth Clemson freshman to be named All-America.

QB Deshaun Watson had a great receiver, too. Mike Williams caught 98 passes from Watson in 2016! Those catches helped the Tigers win the national championship.

Who will be the next big Clemson star?

Right: After scoring another TD for Clemson, DeAndre Hopkins celebrated with his teammates.

GLOSSARY

conference (KON-fur-enss) a group of schools that play each other in sports

founded (FOWN-ded) created or started

freshman (FRESH-mun) a person in his or her first year at a high school or college

interceptions (in-tur-SEP-shunz) passes caught by the defense

opponents (uh-POH-nents) teams or athletes you play against

pedestal (PED-eh-stul) a column or platform that supports a sculpture

Pro Bowl (PROH BOWL) the NFL's annual all-star game

punter (PUNT-er) a football position that kicks the ball to opponents on fourth down

unranked (un-RANKT) not included in a national list of top college football teams

FIND OUT MORE

IN THE LIBRARY

Jacobs, Greg. *The Everything Kids' Football Book*. New York: Adams Media, 2018.

Kaminski, Leah. *Clemson Tigers*. New York: Weigl, 2020.

Sports Illustrated for Kids. *The Greatest Football Teams of All Time*. New York: Sports Illustrated Kids, 2018.

ON THE WEB

Visit our website for links about the
Clemson Tigers:
childsworld.com/links

Note to Parents, Teachers, and Librarians: We routinely verify our Web links to make sure they are safe and active sites. So encourage your readers to check them out!

INDEX

Alabama 11
Atlantic Coast
   Conference 8, 15,
   16, 19, 20
Boyd, Tajh 16, 20
Etienne, Travis 19
Germany 19
Heisman, John 7
Hopkins, DeAndre 20
Howard, Frank 8, 12,
   15
Howard's Rock 12
Kinard, Terry 19

Lawrence, Trevor 11, 16
LSU 16
McFadden, James 19
Memorial Stadium 5,
   15
Notre Dame 11
Riggs, Walter 7, 15
South Carolina 7, 12
Swinney, Dabo 8
Watkins, Sammy 20
Watson, Deshaun 16,
   20
Williams, Mike 20

ABOUT THE AUTHOR

K.C. Kelley is the author of more than
100 sports books for young readers, including
numerous biographies of famous athletes. He went
to the University of California–Berkeley, but his
Golden Bears didn't quite make it into this series!